Alma Falls Awake

With Her Friend

Alma Falls Awake
With Her Friend

story by Sarah Warner
watercolors by Julia Lunk

Blue Tree
PORTSMOUTH

One night I fell awake,
into my dream. There
I was in the forest with
birds on my head.

There were fireflies buzzing and glowing in the night sky. They flew right past me. I could see their eyes, wide in the moonlit night. At first I was afraid, but then it was day.

It was a rare day. The Moon and the Sun were both in the sky smiling at one another over our big world. The Moon whispered something to the Sun. I did not understand his words. They sounded like the wind. The Sun left the room and it was dark again.

The birds laid an egg on my head, then flew away. The egg was large and heavy, hard to balance. But it made me tall. Taller than two caterpillars standing tail to head. The egg was warm.

My egg began to talk to me. It said, "I am here. Your friend. Inside your egg." It was a little strange that this egg was talking to me. But I was dreaming, remember?

So I listened.

The egg started to wiggle and jiggle. It pushed down hard against my skull. It said, "Here I come!"

My goodness! I heard a loud crack! My ears popped. My heart beat. All of a sudden an enormous black bird flapped his wings over my head. He landed near my feet. Squawk!

"I'm so glad to finally see you," cooed my friend. "I am too," I replied. "Would you like some tea?" I asked. "You must have so much to tell me."

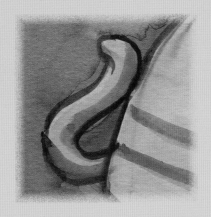

The little girl and her friend talked for a day and a night. They laughed until they cried. They shared all of their secrets.

Night turned into day and my dream ended with the rising, smiling Sun. I missed my friend, but knew I would see him again.

The End.

First published in the United States in 2010
by Blue Tree, LLC
P.O. Box 148
Portsmouth, NH 03802
www.TheBlueTree.com

37 10 1

Printed in Hong Kong

Library of Congress
Cataloging-in-Publication Data
2008935736

Alma Falls Awake With Her Friend
Sarah Warner, Julia Lunk

ISBN-10: 0-9802245-5-1
ISBN-13: 978-0-9802245-5-9

For customer service and orders:
Local 603.436.0831
Toll-Free 866.852.5357
Email sales@TheBlueTree.com

Blue Tree
A BOUTIQUE PUBLISHING FIRM